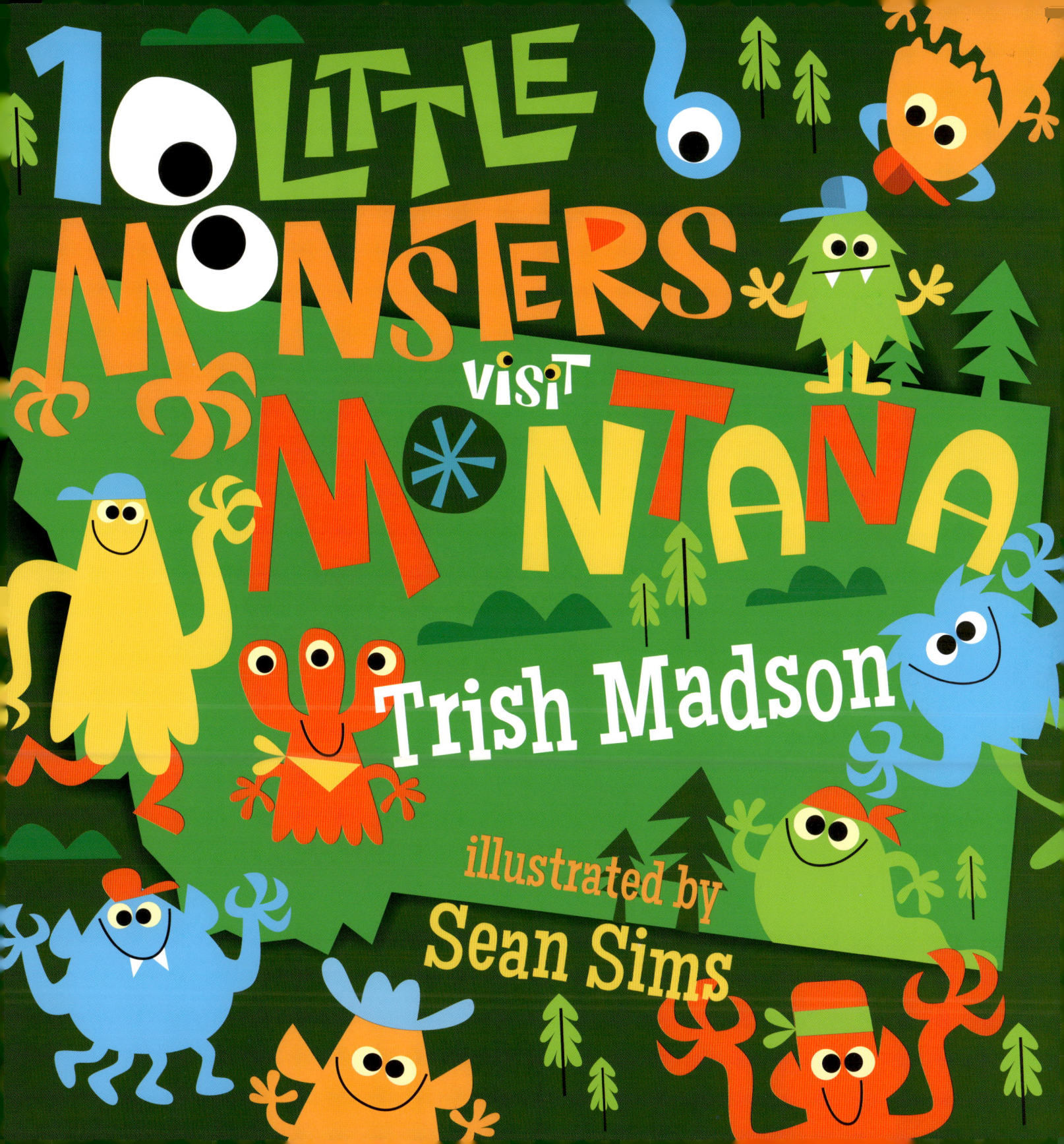

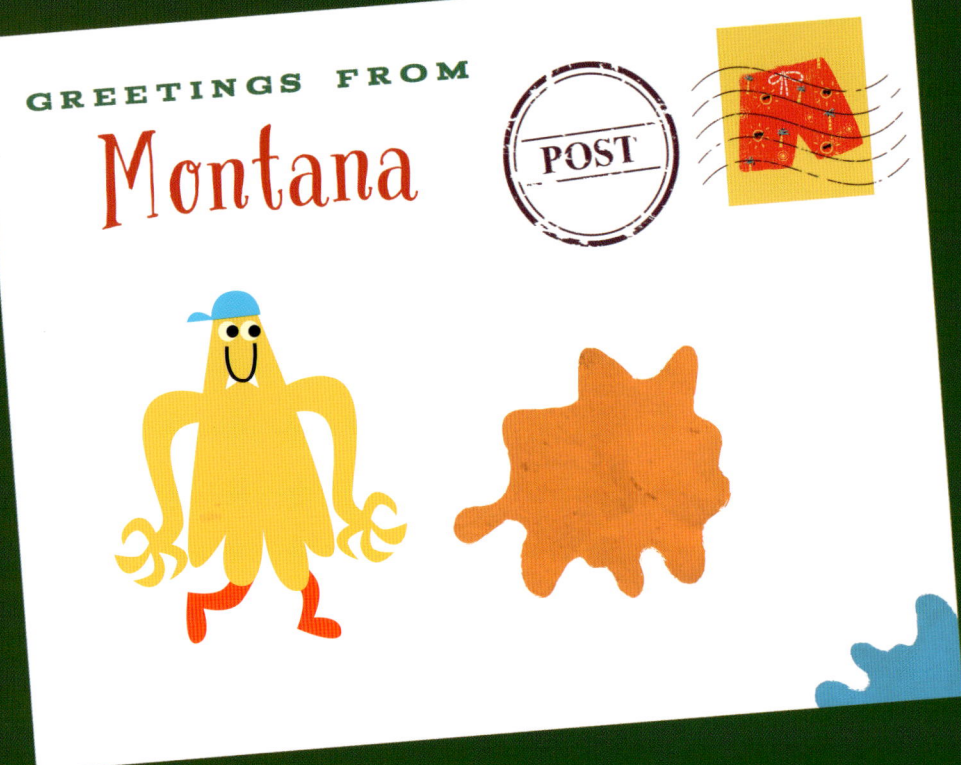

Text copyright © 2020 by Trish Madson
Illustration copyright © 2020 by Sean Sims
All rights reserved.

Published by Familius™ LLC, www.familius.com
1254 Commerce Way Sanger, CA 93657

Familius books are available at special discounts for bulk purchases for sales promotions or for family or corporate use. For more information, contact Premium Sales at 559-876-2170 or email orders@familius.com.

Reproduction of this book in any manner, in whole or in part, without written permission of the publisher is prohibited.

Library of Congress Control Number: 2020935450   ISBN 9781641701945   eISBN 9781641703123

Printed in China

Book and jacket design by Carlos Guerrero
Edited by Maggie Wickes and Brooke Jorden
10 9 8 7 6 5 4 3 2 1

First Edition

10 little monsters, each wearing a bandana, take a trip to the great state of Montana.

10 little monsters, they just can't wait, 'cause monsters love the Treasure State.

Montana is called the Treasure State because it is rich in minerals. The state motto, Oro y Plata, means "silver and gold" in Spanish.

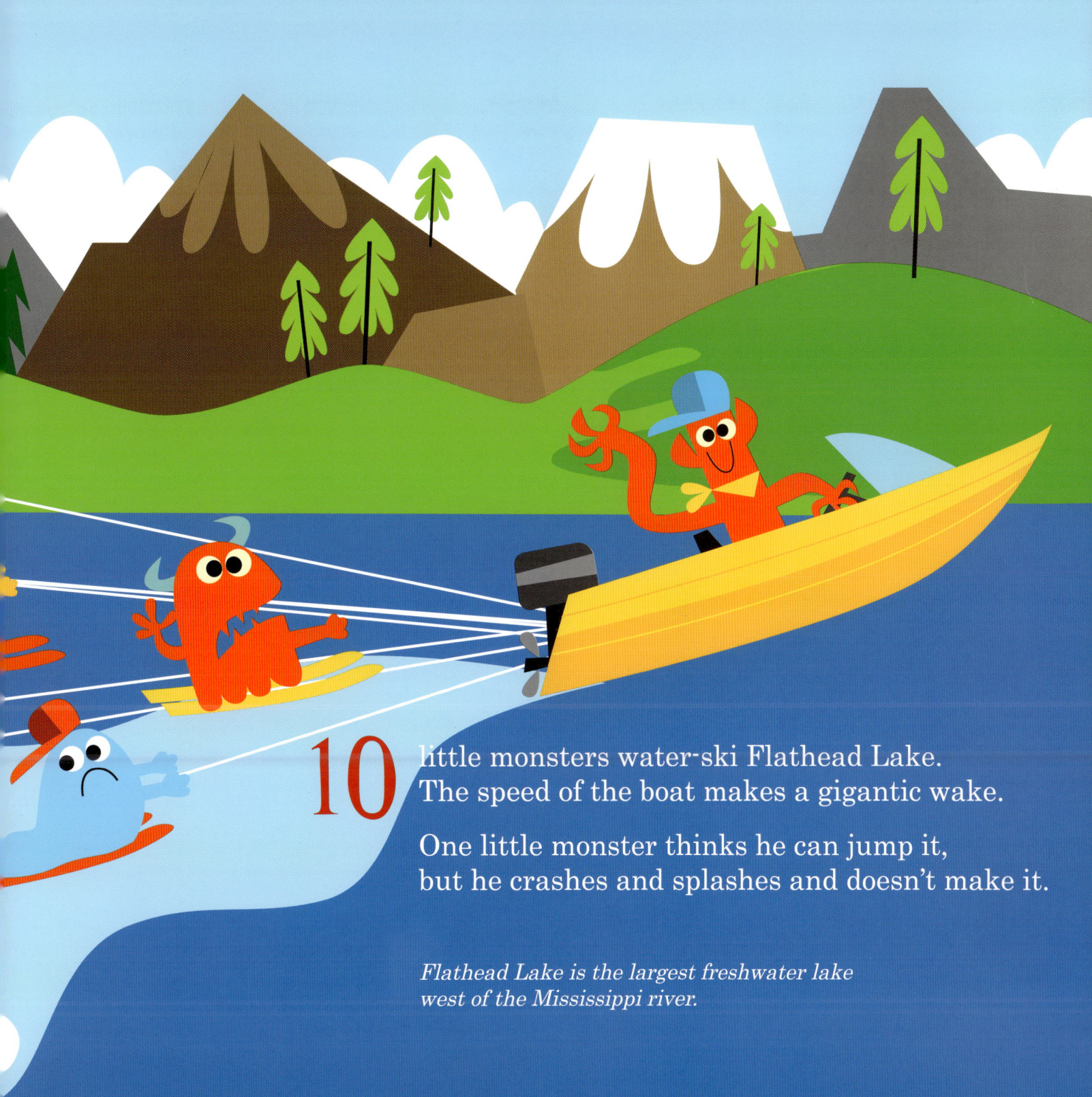

10 little monsters water-ski Flathead Lake.
The speed of the boat makes a gigantic wake.

One little monster thinks he can jump it,
but he crashes and splashes and doesn't make it.

Flathead Lake is the largest freshwater lake west of the Mississippi river.

9 little monsters bike on Going-to-the-Sun Road.
One leads the way and all the rest follow.

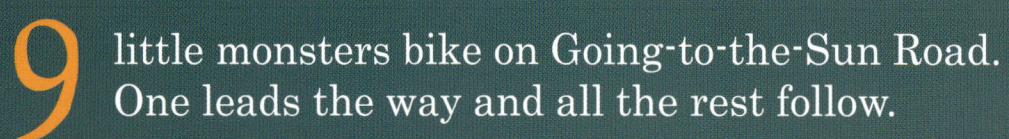

One little monster's bike tire blows out;
now he's on a downhill route.

Going-to-the-Sun Road is 6,646 feet high! It takes two hours to drive the full road by car without stopping.

8 little monsters hike through Ross Creek Cedars, where they all take turns playing follow-the-leader.

One little monster gets ahead of the pack; now he's all alone and can't find his way back.

Some trees in the Ross Creek Cedars grove are more than 400 years old. Many of the trees were growing before Columbus came to America.

7 little monsters race snowmen in Bozeman, throttles pushed down, going as fast as they can.

One little monster tries to take the lead, but he flies off the trail at a very high speed.

In 1887, the largest snowflake ever observed was found in Montana. It was 15 inches across!

6 little monsters visit the Grizzly & Wolf Discovery Center. They get a special tour from the park's director.

The average pack of wolves has 5–8 pack members but can have as many as 30. Montana wolves were once endangered, but thanks to conservation, their numbers are increasing each year.

One little monster wants to run with the pack.
He has lots of fun and can't wait to come back.

4 little monsters discover the Museum of the Rockies.
They see dinosaurs, the planetarium, and illustrated stories.

One little monster leans against Big Mike's foot—
bones crash to the ground; now that monster's kaput.

The Museum of the Rockies covers over 500,000,000 years of history and has the largest collection of dinosaur remains in the US.

3 little monsters camp in Glacier National Park.
They build a nice fire 'cause they're afraid of the dark.

One little monster wanders off on his own.
Now his whereabouts are mysteriously unknown.

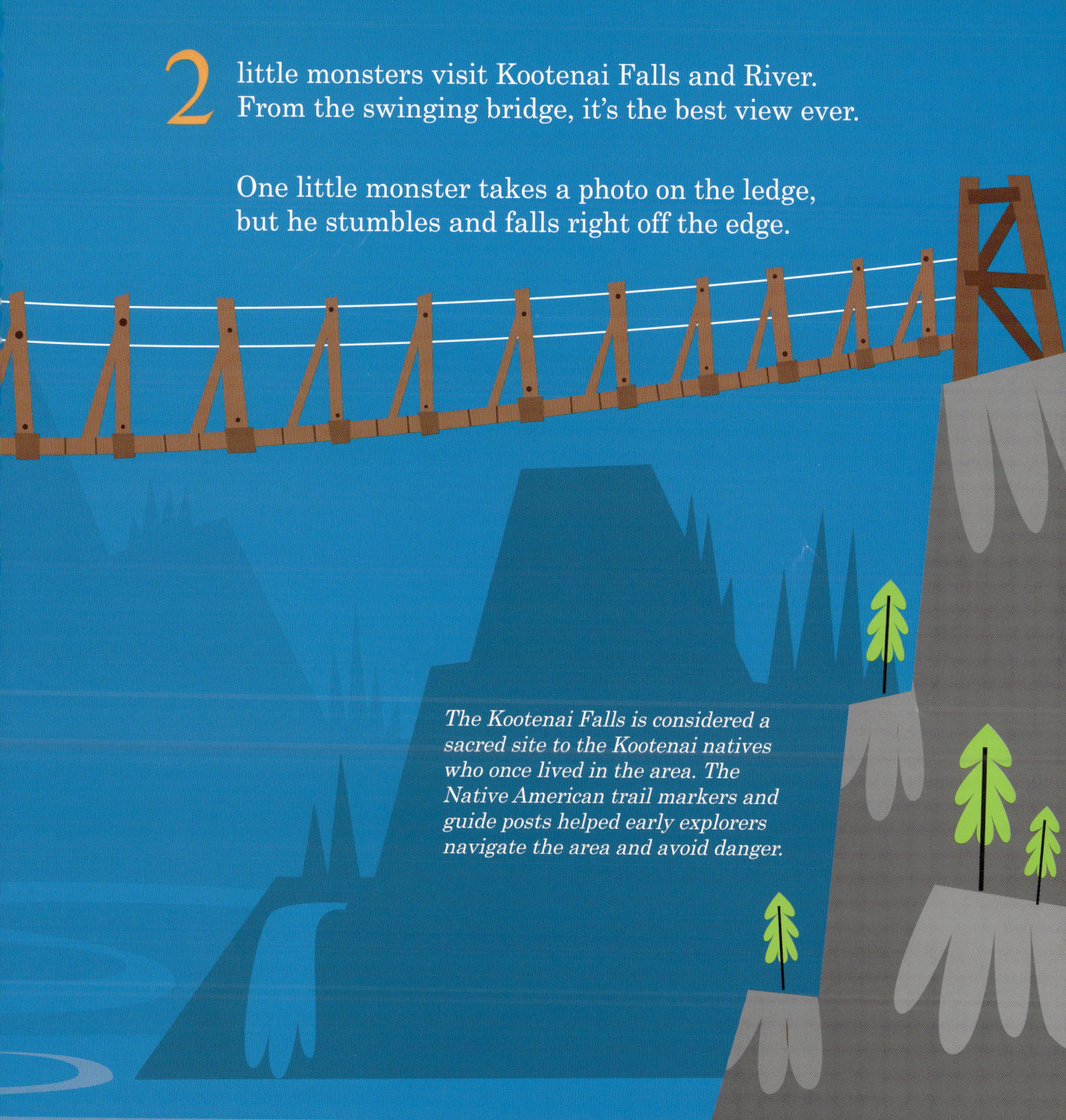

2 little monsters visit Kootenai Falls and River. From the swinging bridge, it's the best view ever.

One little monster takes a photo on the ledge, but he stumbles and falls right off the edge.

The Kootenai Falls is considered a sacred site to the Kootenai natives who once lived in the area. The Native American trail markers and guide posts helped early explorers navigate the area and avoid danger.

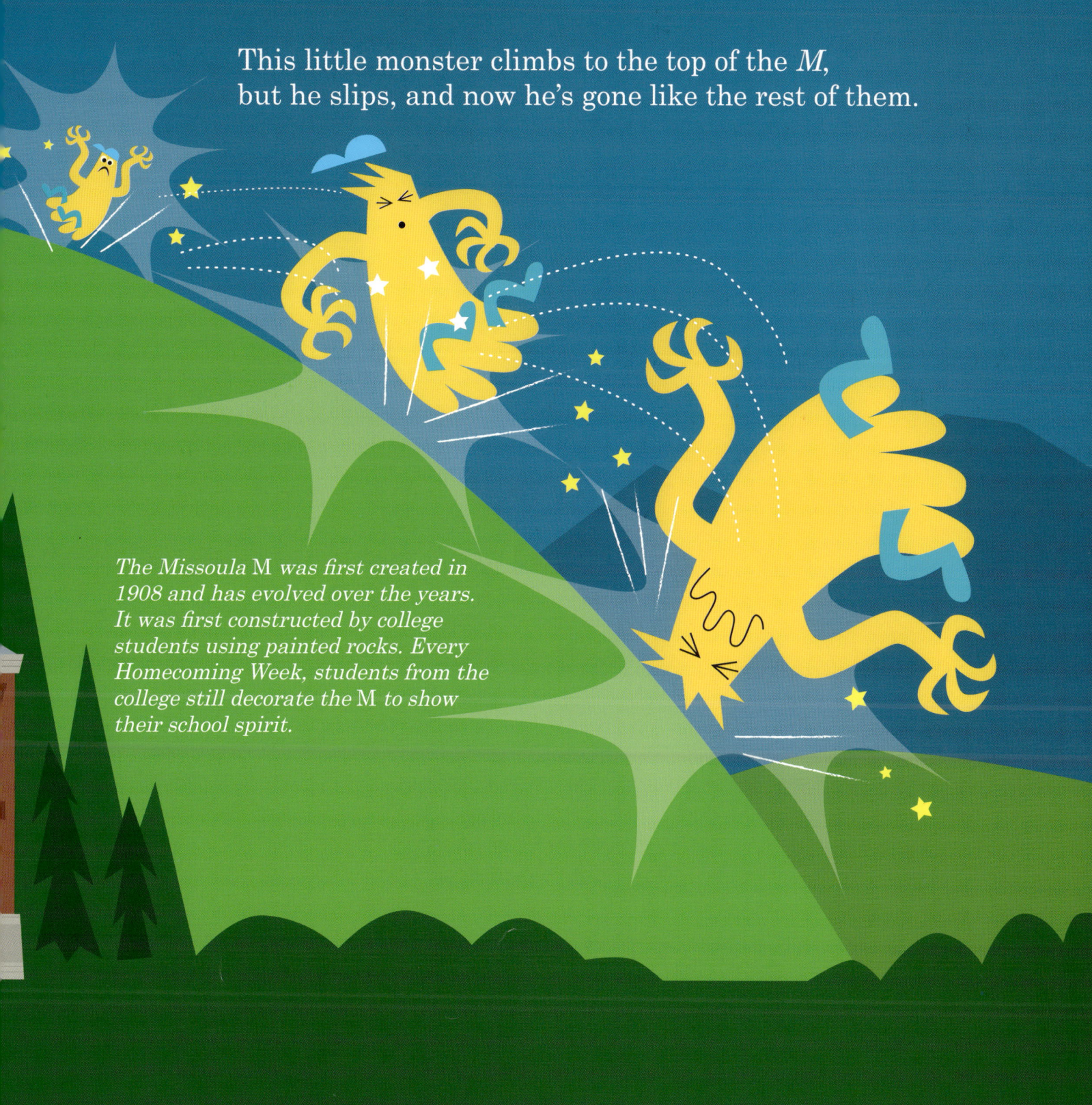

This little monster climbs to the top of the *M*, but he slips, and now he's gone like the rest of them.

The Missoula M was first created in 1908 and has evolved over the years. It was first constructed by college students using painted rocks. Every Homecoming Week, students from the college still decorate the M to show their school spirit.